Pizza Pokey

Written by Jeffrey Stoodt

Illustrated by Jim Durk

STECK-VAUGHN
COMPANY
ELEMENTARY • SECONDARY • ADULT • LIBRARY

You get a mixing bowl.

You pour some flour out.

You pour some water in,

And you mix it all about.

You do the Pizza Pokey,

As you turn the bowl around.

That's what it's all about!

3

You roll the dough all up.

You roll the dough all out.

You use a rolling pin,

And you flatten it about.

You do the Pizza Pokey,

As you spin the dough around.

That's what it's all about!

5

You put the pizza sauce on.

You spread the pizza sauce out.

You put more pizza sauce on,

And you spread it all about.

You do the Pizza Pokey,

As you pour the sauce around.

That's what it's all about!

7

You put some bacon on.

You get more bacon out.

You put more bacon on,

And you sprinkle it about.

You do the Pizza Pokey,

As you turn the pie around.

That's what it's all about!

You put some peppers on.

You get more peppers out.

You put more peppers on,

And you sprinkle them about.

You do the Pizza Pokey,

As you turn the pie around.

That's what it's all about!

You put some sausage on.

You get more sausage out.

You put more sausage on,

And you sprinkle it about.

You do the Pizza Pokey,

As you turn the pie around.

That's what it's all about!

You put some cheese on.

You get more cheese out.

You put more cheese on,

And you sprinkle it about.

You do the Pizza Pokey,

As you turn the pie around.

That's what it's all about!

You do the Pizza Pokey.

You do the Pizza Pokey.

You do the Pizza Pokey.

That's what it's all about! Yeah!